CH00842356

First published 1996 by Methuen
an imprint of Reed Children's Books
Michelin House, 81 Fulham Road, London SW3 6RB
and Auckland, Melbourne, Singapore and Toronto.

ISBN 1 85591 544 8

Printed in Italy

Hunnypot Library

Winnie-the-Pooh
Piglet is Rescued

From the Stories by A.A. Milne

With new and adapted illustrations
in the style of E.H. Shepard

METHUEN

It rained and it rained and it rained. Piglet told himself that never in all his life, never had he seen so much rain. Days and days and days.

"If only," he thought, as he looked out of the window, "I had been in Pooh's house, or Christopher Robin's house, or Rabbit's house when it began to rain, then I should have had Company all this time, instead of being here all alone, with nothing to do except wonder when it will stop."

And he imagined himself with Pooh, saying, "Did you ever see such rain, Pooh?" and Pooh saying, "Isn't it *awful*, Piglet?" It would have been jolly to talk like this, and really, it wasn't much good having anything exciting like floods, if you couldn't share them with somebody.

For it was rather exciting. The little dry ditches in which Piglet had nosed about so often had become streams, the little streams across which he had splashed were rivers, and the river, between whose steep banks they had played so happily, had sprawled out of its own bed and was taking up so much room everywhere, that Piglet was beginning to wonder whether it would be coming into *his* bed soon.

"It's a little Anxious," he said to himself, "to be a Very Small Animal Entirely Surrounded by Water. And I can't do *anything*."

It went on raining, and every day the water got a little higher, until now it was nearly up to Piglet's window...and still he hadn't done anything.

Then suddenly he remembered a story which Christopher Robin had told him about a man on a desert island who had written something in a bottle and thrown it into the sea; and Piglet thought that if he wrote something in a bottle and threw it in the water, perhaps somebody would come and rescue *him*!

He left the window and began to search his house, and at last he found a pencil and a small piece of dry paper, and a bottle with a cork to it. And he wrote on one side of the paper:

HELP!
PIGLIT (ME)

and on the other side:

IT'S ME PIGLIT, HELP HELP!

Then he put the paper in the
bottle, and he threw the bottle as far
as he could throw and he watched it
floating slowly away in the distance.

When the rain began Pooh was asleep. It rained, and it rained, and it rained, and he slept, and he slept, and he slept. He had had a tiring day. You remember how he discovered the North Pole; well, he was so proud of this that he asked Christopher Robin if there were any other Poles such as a Bear of Little Brain might discover.

"There's a South Pole," said Christopher Robin, "and I expect there's an East Pole and a West Pole, though people don't like talking about them."

Then suddenly he was dreaming. He was at the East Pole, and it was a very cold pole with the coldest sort of snow and ice all over it. He had found a beehive to sleep in, but there wasn't room for his legs, so he had left them outside. And Wild Woozles, such as inhabit the East Pole, came and nibbled all the fur off his legs to make Nests for their Young. And the more they nibbled, the colder his legs got, until suddenly he woke up with an *Ow!* – and there he was, sitting in his chair with his feet in the water, and water all round him!

He splashed to his door and
looked out…

"This is Serious," said Pooh. "I
must have an Escape."

So he took his largest pot of honey
and escaped with it to a broad
branch of his tree, well above the
water, and then he climbed down
again and escaped with another pot
…and when the whole Escape was
finished, there was Pooh sitting on
his branch, dangling his legs, and
there, beside him, were ten pots
of honey…

Two days later, there was Pooh, sitting on his branch, dangling his legs, and there beside him, were four pots of honey.

Three days later, there was Pooh, sitting on his branch, dangling his legs, and there beside him, was one pot of honey.

Four days later, there was Pooh…

And it was on the morning of the fourth day that Piglet's bottle came floating past him, and with one loud cry of "Honey!" Pooh plunged into the water, seized the bottle, and struggled back to his tree again.

"Bother!" said Pooh, as he opened it. "All that wet for nothing. What's that bit of paper doing?"

He took it out and looked.

"It's a Missage," he said to himself, "and I can't read it. I must find Christopher Robin or Owl or Piglet, and they will tell me what this missage means. Only I can't swim. Bother!"

Then he had an idea. He said to himself:

"If a bottle can float, then a jar can float, and if a jar floats, I can sit on the top of it, if it's a very big jar."

So he took his biggest jar, and corked it up.

"All boats have to have a name," he said, "so I shall call mine *The Floating Bear*." And with these words he dropped his boat into the water and jumped in after it.

Christopher Robin lived at the very top of the Forest. It rained, and it rained, and it rained, but the water couldn't come up to *his* house. It was rather jolly to look down into the valleys and see the water all round him, but it rained so hard that he stayed indoors most of the time, and thought about things.

Every morning he went out with his umbrella and put a stick in the place where the water came up to, and every next morning he went out and couldn't see his stick any more, so he put another stick in the place where the water came up to. On the morning of the fifth day he saw the water all round him, and knew that for the first time in his life he was on a real island.

It was on this morning that Owl came flying over the water to say "How do you do?" to his friend Christopher Robin.

"I say, Owl," said Christopher Robin, "isn't this fun? I'm on an island!"

"The atmospheric conditions have been very unfavourable lately," said Owl.

"The what?"

"It has been raining," Owl explained.

"Yes," said Christopher Robin. "It has. Have you seen Pooh?"

"Here I am," said a growly voice behind him.

"Pooh!"

They rushed into each other's arms.

"How did you get here, Pooh?" asked Christopher Robin.

"On my boat," said Pooh proudly. "I had a Very Important Missage sent me in a bottle, and owing to having got some water in my eyes, I couldn't read it, so I brought it to you. On my boat."

With these proud words he gave Christopher Robin the missage.

"But it's from Piglet!" cried Christopher Robin when he had read it. "We must rescue him at once! Owl, could you rescue him on your back?"

"I don't think so," said Owl.

"Then would you fly to him at *once* and say that Rescue is Coming? And Pooh and I will think of a Rescue and come as quick as ever we can."

Owl, speechless for once, flew off.

"Now then, Pooh," said Christopher Robin, "where's your boat?"

"There!" said Pooh, pointing proudly to *The Floating Bear*.

It wasn't what Christopher Robin expected, and the more he looked at it, the more he thought what a Brave and Clever Bear Pooh was. Pooh looked modestly down his nose and tried to pretend he wasn't.

"But it's too small for two of us," said Christopher Robin sadly.

"Three of us with Piglet."

"That makes it smaller still. Oh, Pooh Bear, what shall we do?"

And then this Bear, Pooh Bear, said something so clever that Christopher Robin could only look at him with mouth open and eyes staring. "We might go in your umbrella," said Pooh.

For suddenly Christopher Robin saw that they might. He opened his umbrella and put it point downwards in the water. It floated but wobbled. Pooh got in.

He was just beginning to say that it was all right now, when he found that it wasn't. Then Christopher Robin got in, and it wobbled no longer.

You can imagine Piglet's joy when at last he saw the good ship *Brain of Pooh* (*Captain*, C. Robin; *1st Mate*, P. Bear), coming over the sea to rescue him...

And as that is really the end of the story, I think I shall stop there.